THIS BOOK BELONGS TO

....

BEAUTY AND THE BEAST

Written by Helen Anderton

Illustrated by Stuart Lynch

make believe ideas

Reading together

This book is designed to be fun for children who are gaining confidence in their reading. They will enjoy and benefit from some time discussing the story with an adult. Here are some ways you can help your child take those first steps in reading:

❋ Encourage your child to look at the pictures and talk about what is happening in the story.

❋ Help your child to find familiar words and sound out the letters in harder words.

❋ Ask your child to read and repeat each short sentence.

Look at rhymes

Many of the sentences in this book are simple rhymes. Encourage your child to recognize rhyming words. Try asking the following questions:

❋ What does this word say?

❋ Can you find a word that rhymes with it?

❋ Look at the ending of two words that rhyme. Are they spelled the same? For example, "stem" and "them," and "hair" and "bear."

Reading activities

The **What happens next?** activity encourages your child to retell the story and point to the mixed-up pictures in the right order.

The **Rhyming words** activity takes six words from the story and asks your child to read and find other words that rhyme with them.

The **Key words** pages provide practice with common words used in the context of the book. Read the sentences with your child and encourage him or her to make up more sentences using the key words listed around the border.

A **Picture dictionary** page asks children to focus closely on nine words from the story. Encourage your child to look carefully at each word, cover it with his or her hand, write it on a separate piece of paper, and finally, check it!

Do not complete all the activities at once – doing one each time you read will ensure that your child continues to enjoy the story and the time you are spending together. Have fun!

Once, there was a prince called Wayne
who was selfish, mean, and vain.
"I hate to share!" he'd storm and shout,
"It's worse than eating Brussels sprouts!"

He had no friends – just lots of things
    like toys and jewels and diamond rings.
But what Prince Wayne loved most of all
    were roses from his castle wall.

Wayne's mean neighbor, Witchy Lou,
    secretly liked roses, too.
One day she tried to steal a stem,
    but Wayne cried, "Stop! You can't have them!"

The witch thought, "Wayne will pay for this!"
She cried out in an angry hiss,
"An ugly, hairy beast you'll be
     until true love can set you free!"

She swished her wand six times (at least)
     and Wayne became a snarling beast!
He had black eyes and gruesome hair,
     and claws just like a grizzly bear!

From that day on life wasn't easy –
the sight of Wayne made people queasy.
He soon forgot the witch's spell
and gave up on true love as well.

Some years passed, 'til one cold day
a girl called Beauty passed that way.
Her hair was tied back in a plait,
beneath her favorite woolen hat.

She saw the roses, pink and red.
"I think I'll pick one!" Beauty said.
But just as Beauty plucked a rose,
the beast jumped out, and Beauty froze!

"LEAVE MY ROSES BE," Beast cried.
"Please don't eat me!" she replied.
Said Beast, "You took a rose for free –
to pay me back, stay here with me!"

The girl decided to be brave
(the beast looked fairly well-behaved).
So she followed Beast inside –
but what a sight then met her eyes!

In the hall, the walls were ripped;
  the wooden floors were stained and chipped.
Beast looked sadly at his paws.
  "I rip everything with these claws!"

"Poor Beast, I'll help you!" Beauty cried,
and went to find two sticks outside.
She pulled her woolen hat to bits,
and then the girl began to knit.

Soon Beauty joined the beast downstairs.
She said, "I've solved your rips and tears!"
She gently picked up Beast's four paws,
and put a mitten on each claw!

Beast was thrilled! He ran around,
gently padding on the ground.
Nothing scratched or ripped straight through –
his paws were safe, and toasty, too!

He plucked some roses off the wall
and said to Beauty, "Have them all!"
With a shock, young Beauty knew:
She loved him – and he loved her, too!

24

In a flash and with a BOOM,
   the handsome prince was in the room.
Love had broken Lou's cruel spell,
   and cured Wayne's selfishness as well!

25

What happens next?

Some of the pictures from the story have been mixed up! Can you retell the story and point to each picture in the correct order?

Rhyming words

Read the words in the middle of
each group and point to the other
words that rhyme with them.

had

sing

ring

thing

will

cat

said

hat

some

that

nose

pink

rose

those

took

ball

hall

wall

knew

met

claw

girl

paw

saw

year

gone

here

spell

shell

well

Now choose a word and make up a rhyming chant!

The **cat** likes **that hat!**

Key words

These sentences use common words to describe the story. Read the sentences and then make up new sentences for the other words in the border.

Prince Wayne **was** selfish.

Witchy Lou wanted to **have** a rose.

Lou swished **her** wand.

Wayne turned into **a** beast!

When Beauty took a rose, the beast jumped out.

like · very

· his · but · saw · with · all · we · asked · was · go · he

Beast **asked** Beauty to stay with him.

Beast looked at **his** paws.

Beauty **made** mittens for the beast.

Beast gave roses **to** Beauty.

Beauty knew **they** loved each other.

the · and · a · to · not · in · he · I · of · it · have · got · they · on · she · is · for · at

could · when · there · put · this · made · so · be ·

Picture dictionary

Look carefully at the pictures and the words.
Now cover the words, one at a time.
Can you remember how to write them?

beast

claws

hat

mitten

paw

plait

rose

wand

witch